ALSO BY THOMAS PRIDE

Fever

Mercia

The Baron

King and Country

Zayed

Wonderful Untouchables

THOMAS PRIDE

Ucadia Books Company

Published by Ucadia Books Company, a Delaware stock corporation (File Number 6779670) 901 N Market St #705 Wilmington Delaware 19801.
First edition.

Thomas Pride is the pen name and true ancestor of an Australian based philosopher and writer, who is also the inventor and creator of the Ucadia model.

ISBN 978-1-64419-004-3

When sport helped define history

It has often been said that "sport is the great leveller" –
for it matters little whether we come from privilege or
poverty, only that we know how to play the game. Few
other examples prove this quote to be more true than
in the universal love of cricket throughout India and in
particular during the uncertain and difficult times
leading to independence from the United Kingdom in
the 1930's. A time where politics, religion, economics
and sport found themselves intertwined with what
might become of the future face of India.

Yet in the 1930's, midst the passionate debates as to
the future independence of India, there was no
guarantee that cricket in India would outlast beyond
the end of the British Raj.

Wonderful Untouchables is a heart felt "feel good"
story set in India and England. Of how the future of
peace talks and the destiny of the British Empire came
to rest with the fate of a touring "All India" cricket
team of young men born of the highest privilege of
India and another cricket team from the poorest of
slums of India.

To lovers of good sport everywhere.

I've missed more than 9000 shots in my career. I've lost almost 300 games. 26 times, I've been trusted to take the game winning shot and missed. I've failed over and over and over again in my life. And that is why I succeed.

Michael Jordan

Chapter 1

London 1931. No longer a city of chimneys and pea soup fog, but belching motor vehicles and chain smokers. Outside the classic Georgian white lines of Whitehall, was one fellow, swallowed up by an ill fitting suit (Cecil Parker). A solitary non-smoker, Parker appeared stuck in a queue at a security checkpoint, clutching a single sheet of paper. While he waited, he continued fidgeting and pacing on the spot, as if perilously close to wetting himself.

As soon as he was through the checkpoint, Parker burst into a flapping gallop, running through office after office, startling secretaries and their managers alike. He hurried past one more secretary to an imposing oak door and pushed it open.

Inside the room, seated behind a classic old wooden desk was the Prime Minister of the United Kingdom and Ireland, (Ramsay MacDonald) with his Principal Private Secretary (Robert Vansittart) and the Lord Chancellor (Lord (John) Sankey) seated opposite. As Cecil Parker tumbled through the door, all three men appeared startled, with Vansittart and Lord Sankey swivelling their heads around in their chairs to see the source of the commotion.

"He's done it! Irwin's done it Prime Minister," gushed Parker as Prime Minister Ramsay MacDonald belatedly raised his hand up to try and stop him.

"Slow down Parker. Deep breaths," he sighed.

Vansittart tilted his head, as if to stretch a tight muscle, before he shifted his body around uncomfortably to stare with venom at Parker.

"For the love of country man. This is not some racetrack."

A chuckle from Lord Sankey appearing to momentarily relish the sudden discomfort of his colleague.

"R.G. Don't you know, Parker here has the current land speed record for Whitehall."

The briefest of smiles washed over the face of Ramsay MacDonald before he pursed his lips and frowned at Parker.

"Spit it out Parker."

Parker sheepishly advanced and handed the scrunched up piece of paper to Ramsay MacDonald who at first looked at the crumpled ball of paper with a sigh, before starting to flatten it out with his hands. Before he has finished, Parker blurts out the message.

"Prime Minister, an Official telegram from The Foreign Office and India. Lord Irwin has just successfully negotiated an end to the national strikes with Mr Gandhi."

"Thank God," sighed MacDonald.

"Hallelujah," chirped Lord Sankey.

"Well it is about damn time," grumbled Vansittart, still stretching his neck.

"That's one less headache," agreed MacDonald, as he got up from his chair to stare briefly out the window, before turning back to look at Lord Sankey and Vansittart still seated and briefly at Parker hovering in the background. "Now, if I can only stop the banks from collapsing in the next few days, this might be a better week."

MacDonald turned and looked out the window again before looking back at Vansittart. "So what do we do now R.G? We can't keep stalling the Indians forever."

"I am not so sure," responded Vansittart.

An awkward silence before Lord Sankey spoke up. "How about a Knighthood for the little fellow?"

Both Ramsay MacDonald and Vansittart stared hopelessly at Lord Sankey.

"He's trying to get rid of us, not become one of us John," moaned Vansittart.

Another awkward silence followed before Ramsay MacDonald, Vansittart and Lord Sankey all turned to stare at Parker, who at that moment appeared visibly frightened at his continued presence being discovered, like a deer stumbling in its last moment. Ramsay MacDonald waved his arm at Parker.

"Thank you Parker. That will be all. A little less drama next time."

Parker appeared visibly relieved and scurried out of the room.

"How about a Round Table Conference?" asked Vansittart.

Ramsay MacDonald shook his head. "You're not seriously suggesting we start negotiating self rule for India?"

"No. Nothing like that," said Vansittart. "But a Conference here in London gives us a chance to stretch it out a bit. Appeal to good will and all of that. Get some nice photographs and make everyone feel like they have had a good go of it."

MacDonald looked down again at the piece of paper and then at Vansittart. "But why would they come in the first place?"

"Oh, I'm not so sure they won't come," replied Vansittart. "Make a big song and dance of it. Get the

Chapter 1

King to open the conference. People always like to meet Kings, even if they hate the King's men. Make them feel important and equal. Get some senior representatives of the government to greet them as they get off the boat."

"Like whom?" asked Lord Sankey.

"Like you John," grinned Vansittart.

"Hold your horses R.G. If you think I am going to stand on some podium, shaking hands and nodding heads for every colonialist that wants my guts for garters, then -"

MacDonald interrupted him. "It's not such a bad idea R.G."

"But Baldwin, Chamberlain, Churchill and the others will hate it," replied Lord Sankey.

Vansittart was now positively joyous. "Exactly. Hate it. Indeed."

MacDonald thumped the desk as a smile finally cracked open on his face. "Excellent idea then."

Wonderful Untouchables

Chapter 2

Passenger Terminal

A group of British officials, led by lord chancellor Lord (John) Sankey were standing on a platform at the Southampton passenger terminal, smiling for the photographers and cameras. In front of them, a recently arrived ocean liner continued to disembark passengers. A News Announcer spoke loudly as the cameras recorded the scene.

"A historic day for friendly relations between Great Britain and India as representatives of the Prime Minister and His Majesty King George the Fifth welcome the Indian delegation to England."

The line of Indian dignitaries and officials continued from the ocean liner and snaked its way to the location of Lord Sankey and other officials, busily shaking hands and smiling. The News Announcer continued.

"The Round Table talks follow the historic pact between His Majesty's Government and the Indian National Congress led by Mr Gandhi who agreed to end the strikes and boycotts of British made goods that have crippled India and caused tens of thousands of hard working decent men and women to lose their jobs in places as diverse as Manchester and Liverpool."

Lord Sankey continued to shake the hands of the long line of Indian dignitaries, as the unmistakable form of Mahatma Gandhi was escorted away in the background to a waiting car. Lord Sankey looked to his left at his private secretary Martin Coglan.

"How many members of the Indian National Congress did we invite again?" he whispered.

"All of them," replied Coglan.

****

Inside a classic British hall of polished wood, stone walls and stained glass. Standing at a podium on stage at the front of the hall was the King (King George V). Yet only the back and outline of the King at a podium was visible, as his figure was eclipsed by the lights shining down upon him.

"Our Empire has always been forged upon common interests and common goods, not on those issues that divide us," said the King. "And so upon this historic occasion and meeting of delegates of my government of the United Kingdom and Ireland to my right."

Chapter 2

To the right of the King, jammed into pews, like English boarding schoolboys on Easter morning, were rows of grey haired men, led by Prime Minister Ramsay MacDonald sitting sombrely.

"And those representing the interests of the Dominions of India to my left," said the King.

To the left of the King, were mostly empty pews, with just a handful of Indian delegates spread evenly.

"Let me conclude," said the King, "that We wish all representative parties engage in good faith, without prejudice and for the common good of our Sovereign and Commonwealth. So help me God."

The British delegation repeated the words in unison.

"So help us God."

Ramsay MacDonald, looked to his right and whispered to Lord (John) Sankey. "Where the hell is Gandhi ?"

****

Round Table Conference

A clearly annoyed king was escorted out of the main hall. He was followed by a steady stream of British delegates looking like they had just attended a funeral. Outside the doors to the conference, the King stepped into a Rolls Royce flying the royal standard and the car pulled away. A News Announcer spoke over the scene.

"Shocking news for the Government today after Mr Gandhi and most of the Indian delegations boycotted the Round Table Conference after the Government refused to include in the discussions the plight and future of the millions of poor and disenfranchised people in India, Mr Gandhi calls the 'Children of God' or more commonly known as the 'Untouchables'. Instead, Mr Gandhi chose to meet representatives of the workers and unions of Manchester and Liverpool badly affected by the recent protests and bans on purchasing English textiles and goods by Indians as part of their push for self rule. Mr Gandhi even had the chance to watch a local cricket match between workers."

****

Manchester

In Manchester, Mahatma Gandhi and Indian delegates watched local children playing a game of cricket, as the media continued to film and take photographs. To the side of the throng was the personal secretary to Mahatma Gandhi, Venkata Kalyanam with the Lord Mayor of Manchester Mayor George Titt and Coal Mining Union Boss David Caldwell.

"They love him," beamed the Mayor. "If I could get even a third of these people to show me this kind of enthusiasm, I would be a sure thing to stay Mayor."

"George, we all know you'd sell your own kidney if you thought there was a quid in it," added David Caldwell, to collective chuckles from the locals present, except Venkata Kalyanam.

"M. K. Gandhi did not do this to promote politics," said Venkata Kalyanam, shaking his head, "but as a gesture of his solidarity with the ordinary working people who have been so badly affected in the struggle for those basic human rights that all people are entitled to have."

"See! That's what I mean," replied the Mayor. "Beautiful. Powerful, Big Picture stuff. Nothing about boring rates, roads, pubs and shelters."

"Everyone has a part to play Mr Lord Mayor," added Venkata Kalyanam, looking a little concerned.

"What about a cricket match?" asked David Caldwell.

Venkata Kalyanam relaxed his expression. "M. K. Gandhi very much enjoyed watching your local workers cricket team."

"Yes, but what I meant was that the Mahatma mentioned the oppressed and downtrodden workers," said David Caldwell. "You know the 'untouchables'."

"We prefer the term Harijan or Children of God," responded Venkata Kalyanam.

"Right the Children of God," said David Caldwell. "What if a team of them came across and play our team? It would be a great story and symbol of unity between working people."

"That's a cracker of an idea Caldwell!" boomed the Mayor. "I can see it now, The Workers Test. Brilliant!"

"I am not so sure," replied Venkata Kalyanam looking more stressed than ever. "The Harijan are very hard workers and it may not be possible to find a suitable team. But I will pass your suggestion onto M.K. Gandhi and we will endevour to accept the kind invitation."

David Caldwell slapped Venkata Kalyanam on the back. "As soon as you do accept, we will organise the friendly match," he said. "Maybe not George, but the Textile Workers and Coalminer Unions will back the idea. Let's give the little guys a chance to stand in the sun for a change."

"On this observation Mr Mayor, we are all in agreement," smiled Venkata Kalyana politely.

Wonderful Untouchables

Chapter 3

Buckingham Palace, London

The enormous and opulent image of Buckingham Palace at the changing of the guard.

King George V in his full regalia stomped unceremoniously along a corridor and into a beautiful gold encrusted room, followed by his attendant Robert Mallory. The king stopped in front of a sofa and screen and started to unbutton his jacket and then try to pull it off.

"Get this rubbish off me," the King protested. "It will be the death of me."

Mallory started to help the King take off his jacket as the Royal Butler stepped forward to assist.

"Yes your majesty," replied Robert Mallory calmly.

The jacket now off, King George swung around and gave Mallory a deadly stare.

"What a bloody shambles that was. I have never been more embarrassed in my entire bloody life."

The King undid his belt and let the belt and sword fall with a thud to the floor.

"Your Majesty," repeated Robert Mallory, continuing a careful and soothing tone.

"I mean, what lunatic or bunch of idiots arranges a Peace Conference and forgets to invite the other side?" growled the King.

"Your Majesty," said Robert Mallory, "the Prime Minister is waiting to see you as requested."

"Ah, yes, speak of the Devil -"

"But Your Majesty is not fully dressed," added Robert Mallory.

The King scowled at him. "Dressed or undressed, I am still the bloody King."

Mallory and then the Royal Butler nod sheepishly before Mallory hurried away. In the meantime, the butler retrieved the belt and sword from the floor and disappeared. The King sat down on the sofa with his shirt out, suspenders exposed and jacket off, as the Prime Minister entered the room.

"Your Majesty, on behalf of your government," said Prime Minister Ramsay MacDonald. "I express my heartfelt regret at-"

The King put his hand up, cutting off the Prime Minister.

"Yes, Yes, spare me all that dribble Prime Minister. Get to it man. Spit it out. You screwed it up."

"Yes, Your Majesty."

"You stuffed its gizzards man. You blew it. "

Ramsay MacDonald was still looking blankly at the King.

"The Conference thing over India," yelled the King. "Where in the hell was that Gandhi fellow?"

"In Manchester your Majesty."

"Bloody Manchester. Whose head shall I have for this? Yours? Baldwin? Bloody Churchill?"

"I am the Prime Minister of the National Government your Majesty. If anyone is to resign, then I offer my resignation to you forthwith."

King George waved his hand negatively as he moves over to the window and looks out.

"That's the problem with you MacDonald. If Baldwin was standing there, he'd throw a whole convent of nuns under a train before he'd offer his own head. No. Better you stay where you are. There's enough problems without people speculating on another general bloody election."

"Thank you, your Majesty."

"But one more bloody disaster. One more cock up and I will be personally stuffing you as the Christmas Turkey for Balmoral, you hear?"

"Yes Your Majesty. No more cock ups. I assure you."

Chapter 3

****

Westminster Palace

The magnificent backdrop of Westminster Palace. Lord (Stanley) Baldwin, the leader of the Conservative Party and temporary "ally" in the national government was speaking with fellow conservative Chancellor of the Exchequer Neville Chamberlain under one of the main arches of Westminster.

"Never underestimate the public desire for status quo Neville, smiled Lord Baldwin. "Peace in our time, as they say."

"Right, Right you are Stanley," replied Neville Chamberlain. "I'll remember to use that sometime. Peace in our time. Whatever keeps the great unwashed at bay."

Just then a younger man (Ronald Waterhouse) came bounding up to both men.

"My Lords," said Ronald Waterhouse excitedly.

"What is it Waterhouse?" said Lord Baldwin. "You're more excited than usual. Let me guess."

"The Prime Minister wants to nationalize the banks or start handing out welfare to poor people," replied Ronald Waterhouse.

Both Lord Baldwin and Neville Chamberlain started laughing amongst themselves.

"Stanley, your priceless," chuckled Neville Chamberlain.

Lord Baldwin stopped laughing and stared at Waterhouse who looks at Lord Baldwin, then at Neville Chamberlain and then back at Lord Baldwin.

"For goodness sake man," said Lord Baldwin, "he may be Chancellor of the Exchequer, but he is also a conservative."

Waterhouse nodded. "I have it on the highest authority my Lords that the Prime Minister was given a right royal bollocking by the King," he said enthusiastically. "One more mistake and King George has threatened to force an immediate election."

"Not too soon I hope," added Neville Chamberlain. "I'm praying to wash my hands of all this recession mess and get away for a few weeks."

"Now, Now Neville," smiled Lord Baldwin.

Baldwin waved Waterhouse off and he scampers away across the polished floors.

Chapter 3

"In time, all good things come to those who wait," said Lord Baldwin.

****

10 Downing St

Inside 10 Downing Street, Ramsay MacDonald was pacing up and down near the closest window to his desk. Opposite him was his secretary Rose Rosenberg, sitting with a stenographers pad, while Lord John Sankey looked on.

"As a matter of urgency, stop," said Ramsay MacDonald. "I hope and trust Mr President that you are in agreement with the urgency of this proposed currency conference and -"

Suddenly Robert Vansittart poked his head into the room and MacDonald waved him away.

"Not now Robert," grumbled Ramsay MacDonald.

Robert Vansittart withdrew and closed the door.

"Rose, where was I?" asked Ramsay MacDonald.

"The future of Europe and the global financial system requires we act as a matter of urgency, stop," repeated Rose Rosenberg. "I hope and trust Mr

President that you are in agreement with the urgency of this proposed currency conference and -"

"Surrender to us your Wall Street pirates -" interrupted Lord Sankey.

"Enough," said Ramsay MacDonald. "I already have a headache."

Ramsay MacDonald put his hand to his head.

"No, No. And await your earliest reply, stop," added Ramsay MacDonald. "You know the rest Rose. Bla, bla etc.."

Rose got up from her chair and walked to the door to her office.

"And see that the Ambassador to the United States also gets a copy as soon as it is ready," said Ramsay MacDonald.

"Yes Prime Minister," said Rose Rosenberg, closing the door behind her.

"I have an idea about India," said Lord Sankey.

"John, Please tell me it doesn't involve the King," sighed Ramsay MacDonald.

"Well, no. Not really," mumbled Lord Sankey, "but kind of."

"Now you are starting to sound like Baldwin speaking to a constituent," said Ramsay MacDonald.

Chapter 3

"Sorry Prime Minister," said Lord Sankey. "What I meant was, the plan."

"And the plan is?" asked Ramsay MacDonald.

"Invite the Indians to play at Lords as a Test Match," said Lord Sankey.

"That's it?" added Ramsay MacDonald. "That's your plan to save the British Empire from collapse? To invite the Indians to play at the sacred home of cricket?"

"After the next Round Table Conference," said Lord Sankey.

"Now I am really confused," said Ramsay MacDonald.

"The Indians love cricket. They're mad for it," said Lord Sankey. "They play it in the slums and in the palace gardens of the most powerful of maharajas. Maybe one day, they might even be the most important home for cricket."

"I doubt it, but go on," added Ramsay MacDonald.

"Anyway, why not host a test between India and England at the conclusion of the next proposed Round Table Conference?" asked Lord Sankey. "The Indians and the Indian National Congress Party and Mr Gandhi will be forced to participate, otherwise they will be offending their own people."

"And where does the King fit into this?" asked Ramsay MacDonald.

"We invite him to the Test," said Lord Sankey enthusiastically, "to meet both teams and of course all the Indian delegation will have to come as well."

Ramsay MacDonald rubbed his chin, looking out the window. "It might just work," he said. "But John, if this one goes up in smoke like Vansittart's first conference, we are all finished."

Chapter 3

Chapter 4

Bombay 1931

A boy clutching a letter, darted between trucks and cars, midst the cacophony of city life. He ran down an alley that opened up to a road in front of a Cricket stadium. At the main entrance, a security guard stopped the boy and looked at the front of the letter, before letting him through.

Inside the stadium, the boy hurried along a corridor and then up some stairs until he got to a dark glass door with the writing *BCCI - Board of Control for Cricket in India*. He knocked first then opened the door.

Inside the reception area to the office, the boy handed the envelope to a well dressed man (Anthony De Mello), the Secretary to the Board of Control for Cricket in India. De Mello began to open the letter as the boy turned and was almost out the door.

"Boy! Boy! You forgot your coins," he said.

The boy stopped and returned to De Mello who handed him several coins, before the boy nodded appreciatively and left.

An older man (R.E. Grant Govan), the President of the Board of Control for Cricket in India (BCCI), appeared in the reception area and walked over to De Mello.

"What is it?" he asked.

"We have received a letter from Lords," said De Mello.

"The House of Lords, or The Lords?"

"The big one," smiled De Mello excitedly.

"Well, read it out."

De Mello cleared his throat. "The Cricket Club of India and the Board of Control for Cricket in India are cordially invited to field a team of its finest, to attend a test match upon Lords against England.

"It can't be," exclaimed Grant Govan. "Here, give me the letter."

De Mello handed Govan the letter as Govan re-read it whispering to himself. He looked up at De Mello.

"In all my life," said Grant Govan, "I never dreamed of the day that the British would invite me, would invite us, India to play a game of Test Cricket against them."

"They must be desperate," grinned De Mello.

Chapter 4

"What makes you say that? We have some fine cricketers. Some of our best have already played over in England."

"R.E. The British don't send such an invitation in the middle of talks over the future of the government of India for no reason. They must want something."

"Well, whatever it is, I am all ears. Lords De Mello! Lords! Imagine that!"

Grant Govan slapped De Mello on the back. "That reminds me," said De Mello. "You have a meeting with M.K. Gandhi tomorrow."

"Tomorrow? What about?" asked Grant Govan. "Maybe it is about the test?"

De Mello shrugged his shoulders.

"No matter," said Grant Govan. "Yes. Tell his office I will be there."

****

Gandhi Compound

Grant Govan walked through beautifully kept gardens along a path toward a pair of guards and a large doorway within the Gandhi Compound.

As Grant Govan entered the doorway, he was greeted by M.K. Gandhi's Private Secretary Venkata Kalyanam. Grant Govan could see Gandhi himself way off in the distance, sitting on the floor using his thread spinning wheel.

"Welcome Mr Govan," said Venkata Kalyanam politely. "Please have a seat."

Venkata Kalyanam directed Grant Govan to a set of sofas over looking a smaller internal courtyard.

"Mr Govan, M.K. Gandhi wishes to express and relay a message to you from his most recent voyage to England. The English are most keen to see that we accept their invitation to field a side of our finest cricketers."

Grant Govan nodded in agreement. "Bapu is right," he said, "we just received a letter on the very matter yesterday."

"Good," smiled Venkata Kalyanam. "Then you are clear as to the significance and important of this gesture."

"Absolutely clear. Could not be clearer. Crystal clear. Got it."

"The Indian National Congress sees this as a gesture of our strength of self determination. Our ability to resolve our own differences without British interference."

"Certainly, yes," beamed Grant Govan. "That is why I am convening a meeting of a board to select the finest team from our most elite and illustrious cricketers to represent an All Indian team-"

"Of Harijans," said Venkata Kalyanam interrupting him.

Grant Govan looked at him strangely. "Excuse me? What did you say?"

"Children of God," said Venkata Kalyanam. "A Team of the Finest Harijans to play against the finest team from the factories and workhouses of Manchester and Liverpool in England."

"What? Untouchables?"

Venkata Kalyanam stared at Grant Govan who quickly changed his disposition.

"Sorry, Children of God," said Grant Govan sheepishly. "I was referring to the invitation by Lords for India to field a team for a historic test against England."

"Yes, yes, that is all well and good," said Venkata Kalyanam, "but Bapu however assured the British authorities in those cities that a team would be sent in the coming year across to England as a symbol of friendship and solidarity between working people of the two countries."

"Yes, yes, working people. Got it. Untouchables, yes."

Venkata stared at Grant Govan again.

"Sorry, Harijans," smiled Grant Govan nervously. "Sorry, old habit."

"One that M.K. and the Party hopes and prays you will help break for the sake of all of India and the world in doing your duty."

Venkata stood up and extended his hand.

"Yes, yes. I will do what I can. I must," said Grant Govan, continuing to shake the hand of Venkata Kalyanam vigorously. "Please assure Bapu that the whole of cricket in India are 100% behind him."

"Then it is in your capable hands Mr Govan."

****

BCCI Headquarters

Grant Govan was sitting back in a chair in the BCCI Headquarters, with a hand towel resting on his forehead. There was a knock on the door.

Chapter 4

"Not now," sighed Grant Govan, as De Mello stepped into the office.

"What is wrong? How did the meeting with Bapu go?"

Grant Govan sighed as he buried his head in his hands.

"Don't even get me started," moaned Grant Govan. "First it wasn't with Bapu, but his secretary Venkata Kalyanam. Secondly, it had nothing to do with the test at Lords, but finding some damn team of untou... harijans."

"A team of what? untouchables?"

"Please don't say that word, it it will be the death of my career," said Grant Govan. "Yes, children of god."

"I don't understand," said De Mello, shaking his head.

"Apparently M.K. Gandhi made the offer when he was in England. So now we have to find a team."

"We have only a few months to fill the first team to play a Test Match at Lords with England and Gandhi wants us to find a team of dalit?" exclaimed De Mello. "It can't be done!"

"It has to be done," said Grant Govan. "He has made a solemn promise to the British workers."

"But there is no such team?" exclaimed De Mello. "Where are we going to find such a team?"

"Don't you remember that team of boys who beat the local British garrison a few months ago?" asked Grant Govan.

"They were boys. We are talking about men," said De Mello. "Besides, they belong to an orphanage run by the Little Sisters of Charity. They'd never agree."

"That is why I am sending you rather than myself," smiled Grant Govan.

Chapter 5

Bombay Slums

Midst the explosion of colour, activity, work, death and life of the classic slums of India, a car fought its way through the crowd.

The car finally stopped at a wall, with a small plaque saying *Little Sisters Of Charity*. Out of the car stepped Anthony De Mello who walked over to the gate of the compound.

Inside, the compound was a hive of activity of young men playing a game of cricket within the confined space. At the makeshift dirt crease was Parindra Chamar. At the other end of the wicket was Chetan Sadna. Fielding as wicket keeper was Samir Saroj. A young man (Kanan Ram) bowled and Parindra knicked the ball into the air above two other boys Sagar Khade and Bhavesh Makwana.

"Catch him! Catch him!" yelled Kanan Ram.

As Parindra Chamar ran with Chetan Sadna between the wickets, the ball fell between Sagar Khade and Bhavesh Makwana and neither caught it. There was a collective sigh. Sagar Khade threw the ball back to Kanan Ram as the gate opened and Anthony De Mello walked inside.

The boys stopped and watch as Sister Jyoti and Sister Sachita come over to greet him.

"Mr De Mello," smiled Sister Jyoti. "My name is Sister Jyoti and this is Sister Sachita."

"An honour sisters," replied De Mello.

De Mello shook both their hands and then followed Sister Jyoti and Sister Sachita to a room off the side of the courtyard.

"Please come in," said Sister Jyoti.

The two nuns escorted De Mello into a spartan room, dominated by a crude wooden cross at one end and pictures of saints on a side wall. In the room, waiting for them was Sister Varuni. She stood up as De Mello walked into the room.

"Let me introduce Sister Varuni, our Superior," said Sister Jyoti.

De Mello extended his hand to Sister Varuni, then sat down.

"How may we help you Mr De Mello?" asked Sister Varuni.

"I must apologize Mr De Mello," smiled Sister Jyoti, "as our directness may sometimes appear abrupt."

Chapter 5

De Mello shook his head and smiled. "Direct is fine. I wish all people were as direct," he replied. "Sisters, I hear the boys are very good at cricket?"

"Good. They are brilliant!" exclaimed Sister Jyoti. "The best in the whole district of any team, Indian or British."

"Too good," moaned Sister Sachita. "The boys do not spend enough time on their studies."

"They beat the British Garrison. At their own game!" responded Sister Jyoti. "Young Kanan and Ganan are as fine and accurate a pair of bowlers as there is in India."

"You mean the boys actually beat a British cricket team?" asked De Mello excitedly.

"Oh yes," said Sister Jyoti, "and they would have beaten the local Indian district side fairly if the local prince had not been so incensed and ordered half his players to be removed and forfeit the game on technicality."

"Parindra is their leader and hero," said Sister Sachita.

"I'd like to meet young Parindra," replied De Mello as Sister Sachita looked first to Sister Varuni, who nodded approvingly, before getting up from her chair.

"He is like a young C.K. Nayudu," gushed Sister Jyoti, "leading his team to victory."

"That is some claim," smiled De Mello, looking at Sister Sachita who had stopped herself at the door.

"Parindra is no Colonel Nayudu," frowned Sister Sachita. "He is far too humble a boy to be like that puffed peacock. I will go get him."

As Sister Sachita left, De Mello looked back at Sister Varuni. "Alas, a useless skill be this cricket," she said. "For as orphans they'd be better served to learn the skills of making shoes or cleaning floors."

"Maybe not Sister," replied De Mello. "Mahatma Gandhi has requested that a team of Dalit travel to England to play a series of exhibition matches with workers from Manchester and Liverpool."

Sister Varuni shook her head negatively, just as Sister Sachita returned accompanied by Parindra Chamar and Kanan Ram.

"That is all very wonderful of Mr Gandhi, said Sister Varuni, "but as an order we have scarcely enough to pay for essentials. We have no money for such a voyage."

Upon seeing Parindra and Kanan, De Mello got up and extended his hand to both of them.

Chapter 5

"This is Parindra," said Sister Sachita introducing Parindra, "and this is Kanan Ram our fast bowler."

"Parindra. I hear you are as fine a cricketer as Colonel Nayudu. In fact, you look a lot like him, only younger," smiled De Mello. "I am Anthony De Mello, Secretary of the BCCI, the Cricket Board of India."

"It is an honour to meet you Sir, said Parindra nervously. "Thank you Sir Anthony. "

"Mr De Mello is fine Parindra."

"Mr De Mello was sharing with us some of the happenings of M.K. Gandhi when he was in England," added Sister Varuni. "Do you remember Kanan and Parindra the newsreel we showed you all?"

"Yes. Yes, I do," replied Kanan. "Bapu visited the factories of the people in England and they were playing cricket."

"Exactly Kanan," added De Mello. "And that is why I am here. The Cricket Board of India would like to sponsor your team to visit England to represent India and Mahatma Gandhi in playing cricket teams of workers. The Cricket Board of India will pay for the voyage and the accommodation of course."

"Such an unrealistic promise would destroy their hearts," said Sister Sachita.

"No, I assure you indeed it is a genuine offer," replied De Mello. "The Cricket Board of India will pay for your team to accompany us to England to play at an exhibition match with local British community and worker teams."

Parindra looked at Sister Varuni. "Mother can we please go?" he pleaded. "We will do everything you ask."

Sister Varuni looked at Sister Jyoti, who nodded enthusiastically and then at Sister Sachita who shook her head negatively.

"These beautiful boys would be exposed to all the corruptions of the world," she protested.

"Please sister," replied De Mello. "This would be the first and possibly the last time many of these young men may ever leave the slums. If there is no cost, and we keep them safe from any danger, then why would it be so harmful?"

"Because it is not the life they will face when they leave here," snapped Sister Varuni. "It is but a cruel illusion of a world that they will be denied. And I would rather sacrifice such an opportunity to ensure they never suffer such an injury to their beautiful spirits."

"But siste-"

"No!" bellowed Sister Varuni, cutting off De Mello.

Chapter 5

"Mother, please we already know about the world. Why won't you let us see?" pleaded Kanon.

"Because you know nothing of money and you have none. You have no uniforms. You know nothing of self discipline and your study marks are terrible", replied Sister Varuni. "Other than that, everything is fine."

Parindra looked at Sister Varuni sheepishly.

"Can I please have a pencil to write down that list?"

"Don't worry," replied Kanan. "I have memorised it."

Sister Varuni got up from her chair, followed by the two other sisters. "I am sorry Mr De Mello. The boys simply are not yet ready. The answer will have to be no."

Wonderful Untouchables

Chapter 6

Little Sisters of Charity Orphanage

Kanan Ram and Parindra Chamar were sitting at a desk, while a line of boys submit pieces of paper to them. Kanan Ram shook his head negatively.

"No one is even close to writing like Mother Sachita," he moaned.

Parindra smiled. "Patience. It doesn't have to be perfect, just good enough to convince Mr De Mello from Indian Cricket."

"But it won't work," sighed Kanan. "What if we miss the letter coming back?, then it is over."

"Stop moaning and check the writing," said Parindra as Chetan Sadna, submitted his piece of paper.

Kanan looked at it. "Very funny Sadna. Now, show me your copy of the hand writing of Mother Sachita."

"It is my copy," protested Chetan Sadna.

Patrindra looked at it and shook his head.

"Kanan is right. It can't be. It even has the smudging she does with her left hand."

"Exactly," said Chetan Sadna proudly.

"And you did this?" asked Parindra.

"Yes," smiled Chetan. "My family were official notaries to the British colonel, until they brought in their own."

"So you are not an orphan then?" asked Kanan.

Chetan Sedna shook his head negatively.

"No, but my father and uncles have been in prison for forgery since I was very young. They still taught me. What other documents do you need?"

Kanan Ram and Parindra look at one another.

****

Cricket Stadium

The main New Delhi Cricket Stadium and home to the BCCI offices. Grant Govan, Anthony De Mello and twelve other men were sitting around a table now in the centre of the room of the BCCI Office.

De Mello whispered to Grant Govan. "Good news, I received a letter from the Mother Superior of that team in Bombay. They have agreed to travel," he said.

Grant Govan nodded his head, while smiling to the rest of the people in the room. "Excellent, lets speak after the meeting and get planning underway."

Usef Mamri of the Sindh Kanan Mahar then spoke up.

"On behalf of the representatives of Sindh, I motion that the BCCI withdraw from the ICC," said Usef Mamri.

"Mr Mamri we already have a motion on the table for which we are seeking resolution," said De Mello.

"Then I move we suspend standing orders to discuss the formal withdrawal of India from the Imperial Cricket Conference," grinned Usef Mamri

"The United Provinces second the move," interjected Kanan Mahar.

"Order!" shouted Grant Govan. "There will be no hijacking proceedings to discuss the agendas of various patrons thank you. Not until we resolve this issue of the selection of the All Indian Team for England."

"Dr B.R.Ambedkar repudiates the patronage and recognition given to Imperial Britain and its false claims by this body," added Kanan Mahar, "and those who choose to be associated with supporting Britains superiority of cricket."

"You can't be serious Mr Mahar," said Grant Govan in frustration. "You do realise you are the representative of United Provinces, for cricket not rugby or soccer."

"And soccer is precisely the kind of sport that Dr B.R.Ambedkar would very much like to see as our new nations official code," replied Kanan Mahar. "Not some derivative of British Imperialism."

"Hear hear!" shouted Usef Mamri. "The All India Muslim League support Dr Ambedkar on his quest for a national sport that is completely clean from any ties with England. We do not wish our new state under Sharia law to be stained by the prejudices of the British."

"You all realise you are at a cricket ground?" asked De Mello sarcastically. "You are here as members of cricket associations aren't you?"

"Settle down everyone please," said Grant Govan. "Then let us vote on the proposal that we secure the Maharaja of Porbandar as Captain and that we defer the vote on any break of association with the ICC until after this historic Test Match with England."

General nodding around the room.

"And my motion?" asked Usef Mamri.

Chapter 6

"I propose we defer a vote until after the success of the test with England," replied Grant Govan. "All in favor?"

More general nodding around the room.

"But if this test match and tour suggested by Britain turns out to be a trap to embarrass us, then the All Muslim League shall be formally voting to sever all ties with the English and ICC," snapped Usef Mamri.

"So shall the Dalit of Dr Ambedkar," added Kanan Mahar, "including a motion to abolish this body as an anarchism of European colonialism."

"Very well. Very well," said Grant Govan. "We shall see."

"We shall see," snapped Kanan Mahar.

****

Little Sisters of Charity Orphanage

The post boy arrived to the orphanage and was immediately surrounded by Sagar Khade and Kanan Ram.

"Cough them up," said Kanan Ram.

"But I am only supposed to give the mail to Sister Varuni," the post boy protested.

"We went through this three days ago," said Kanan Ram "Do you want the chocolate bars or not?"

The post boy nodded his head and handed over the mail. Kanan Ram gave him two chocolate bars and the post boy ran away. One of the letters was from the official cricket board of India (BCCI). Kanan opened it quickly and read it.

"What does it say?" said Sagar Khade excitedly.

Kanan Ram smiled. "It says we are going to England in three months."

****

Maharaja Palace

The magnificent Indian palace of the Maharaja of Porbandar. An oasis of expansive gardens surrounding a full sized cricket pitch on which two teams were playing.

Under umbrellas, sipping iced drinks were Grant Govan and Anthony De Mello as they watched the game. Suddenly there was a shout from the pitch followed by applause as a batsman (Maharaja Of Porbandar) was bowled out. He walked back from the pitch to where De Mello and Govan were sitting.

"More lemonade?" asked the Maharaja.

Chapter 6

Both men shake their heads.

"Good innings," smiled De Mello.

The Maharaja laughed.

"They are good cricketers, but also fiercely loyal," said the Maharaja. "I demanded our best bowler throw a few down like Jardine at me and the poor fellows burst into tears."

"He is not the only one feeling the pressure," added Grant Govan.

A second shout from the pitch followed by applause.

"That's it. We're all out," said the Maharaja.

Across walked one of the batsmen (Kumar Shri Limbdi) while the other players disperse towards some waiters holding drinks.

"Let me introduce you to my dearest and best friend, his Highness Prince K.S. Limbdi."

Kumar Shri Limbdi shook hands with Grant Govan and Anthony De Mello.

"An honour," said Kumar Shri Limbdi.

"When my father the Maharaja died when I was only seven, I felt my world had ended," said the Maharaja. "That was before I met Kumar at Rajkot and then later his beautiful younger sister Rupaliba."

"Your wife," added Kumar Shri Limbdi.

The Maharaja laughed.

"Yes indeed. In answer to your previous observation R.E., It seems everything is fastening up to some event. Yet I fear it will not all entirely be beneficial to humanity," said the Maharaja, taking a sip of lemonade. "In any case, this invitation to play at Lords is truly a historic honor and major step in the right direction."

Both De Mello and Grant Govan nod.

"We would like you to be Captain of the Indian team."

The Maharaja's face suddenly changed from jovial to sombre.

"A tremendous honour. A historic honour for which I feel uniquely unqualified. Why not C.K. Nayudu our best cricketer? "

"He is a great cricketer," replied Grant Govan.

"Our best," added De Mello. "We have also drafted Mohammad Nissar and Amar Singh, so you will have two of the fastest and most accurate bowlers in the world on your side."

"But this is more than our first test match with England, said Grant Govan. "The very future of our game is at stake."

Chapter 6

"The forces of Al Jouhar and the Indian Muslim League are threatening to split the game. And the forces of Dr.B.R.Ambedkar want to ban it altogether," said De Mello.

"Mohammad Nissar is naturally sympathetic to the proposition of an all Muslim separate state," added Grant Govan, "while C.K. Nayudu is a genius on the turf but a demanding character. So we need someone like you, who is wise to both the world, its politics as well as a love of cricket."

The Maharaja got up and paced around the umbrellas. "Then Kumar shall be my Vice Captain," he said.

"Thank you brother but don't you think C.K. Nayudu would be better suited?" asked Kumar Shri Limbdi.

"If I am to leap into the lions den," smiled the Maharaja, "then I wish to choose those whom I trust will follow me."

The Maharaja extended his hand to Grant Govan and then to Anthony De Mello. He picked up a glass of lemonade and the other men follow.

"There it is gentlemen," said the Maharaja. "To India and to our first test match!"

"To India."

****

10 Downing Street, 1932

The image of the famous door of 10 Downing Street. Inside, Ramsay MacDonald entered his office with Robert Vansittart behind him.

"The Indian conference is all arranged," said Robert Vansittart.

"And the Indian cricket team?" asked Ramsay MacDonald.

"I believe they leave today or tomorrow Prime Minister. They are being led by the Maharaja of Porbandar."

"Here is hoping nothing cocks up this time."

"The Maharaja is sailing here in some floating palace yacht he rented from another Maharaja. Do you want the whole media circus at the passenger terminal?"

"No, no, that's what we did last time and look what happened. Lets get them settled and we can do a photo opportunity outside here at No 10 of them all being greeted by me."

"Good idea Prime Minister."

Chapter 6

"We shall see."

Wonderful Untouchables

Chapter 7

Ocean Liner Passenger Terminal, British India 1932

An ocean liner was in its final preparations to depart the shore. On the wharf, next to the galley onto the ship, were the Maharaja of Porbandar, Grant Govan, Anthony De Mello, K.S. Limbdi and the rest of the India Cricket team including C.K. Nayudu and Amar Singh.

"Is my cabin arranged?" asked C.K. Nayudu expectantly.

"First Class. Only the best for you C.K.," smiled the Maharaja. "We will only be a few days behind you."

C.K. Nayudu nodded as people continue to board the ship.

"So what do you think of the team?" asked De Mello.

"With a years practice and some better players then maybe, just maybe we have a chance."

"Not everyone is as great as you Colonel," added Amar Singh to muffled laughter.

"Laugh all you like you hyenas," responded C.K. Nayudu. "Wait till you get in front of Douglas Jardine. Oh yes. He is not some snotty English gentleman. He will tear you apart, break your nose, or your collar bone if you are lucky. You think the English play rough here. Wait till you see their team on their own home ground."

"See you in England," added the Maharaja.

****

Ocean Liner Passenger Terminal

While the last of the passengers get onto the ocean liner, some crew were finishing loading goods onto the ship. One of the men was coughing terribly.

****

Sisters Of Charity

All was quiet in the Sisters of Charity compound except for a barking dog and some music coming from one of the rooms. Inside, the simple dormitory of bunk beds were arranged like a military camp. A couple of lights were turned on by the side of some of the beds.

"What do you think it will be like?" asked Chetan Sadna.

Chapter 7

"I have seen pictures," replied Kanan Ram. "It is dirty, filthy and full of pick pockets and prostitutes."

"That's Charles Dickens stupid," said Gagan Nayanar to laughter among the boys.

"Parindra, what do you think it will be like?" Gagan Nayanar.

"Go to sleep. Get some rest, replied Parindra. "We're leaving on the ship to England tomorrow."

"Full of Rich English people yelling at each other because they do not have enough Indians to do all the work," added Kanan Ram.

General laughter.

"How can you sleep before such an adventure of a lifetime?" asked Chetan Sadna.

"Easy. I close my eyes and pretend you're not speaking," replied Parindra. "By the way, there are plenty of poor people in England as well as Rich people. You will see."

"Do you think the sisters will find out and stop us?" asked Gagan Nayanar.

"Only if you keep talking. So shut up and get some sleep," grumbled Kanan Ram.

****

Ocean Liner At Sea

The Ocean Liner cut its way through the high seas. Inside the crew quarters, the same men who were loading the ship were now confined to their bunks, grievously ill and coughing.

****

Cargo Ship, Terminal

The young men from the Sisters of Charity walked in single file, led by Gagan Nayanar, along a galley onto an old looking Cargo ship.

"This boat smells like old men and old trucks," complained Gagan Nayanar. "I think I am going to be sick."

"What did you expect your highness?" added Chetan Sadna.

General laughter.

"You've smelt the same thing coming out of the kitchen of Sister Jyoti back at the orphanage," said Chetan Sadna.

"Don't remind me," said Gagan Nayanar. "Now I am going to be sick."

Chapter 7

Yet just as Gagan Nayanar stepped off the top of the galley onto the ship, standing in front of him with the captain were Sisters Jyoti, Sachita and Varuni. Gagan freezes for a moment out of shock, causing a ripple effect with the other boys walking up the galley.

"Careful Gagan you oaf," complained Chetan Sadna, until he also saw the three frowning nuns on the deck of the ship.

"What were you saying about my cooking eh Gagan?" growled Sister Jyoti.

"And you Chetan, creating forgeries of my hand writing," added Sister Varuni, shaking her head.

Parindra stepped forward. "Mother Superior, it is all my fault -"

Sister Varuni put her hand up to stop him speaking. "Parindra, do you honestly think we were oblivious to your plans?"

Parindra shrugged his shoulders.

"We knew you were up to something when your rooms were perfectly tidy and your homework was done," laughed Sister Sachita, causing Sister Varuni to frown at her.

"The ship is about to depart so I won't be long winded, said Sister Varuni. "We wanted you to appreciate the importance of striving for something and not having it simply given to you. I never wanted to deprive you of your dream. The captain here has all your proper paperwork and you have our blessings."

Sister Varuni then stepped over to Chetan Sadna and frowned. "And no more documents Chetan, understand?"

Chetan Sadna nodded nervously.

The Sisters embraced each of the boys and then departed down the galley, back to shore.

****

Ocean Liner Near Coast

The Ocean Liner was now positioned off the coastline of England.

Captain Harrington with his hand over his mouth watched as two bags were sown up in the same crew quarters seen earlier where the same two men were grievously ill.

"They both passed this morning," said Seaman Khamar. "There are five more crew in the engine room and one in the galley all sick."

"All with the same symptoms?" asked Captain Harrington.

Chapter 7

Seaman Khamar nods affirmatively.

"Cholera."

The Captain shook his head as he backed away. He turns to a second officer (Lieutenant Askaya)

"Notify the harbour master at Southampton," said the captain. "Tell him we'll be needing quarantine."

The Lieutenant nodded and left.

****

Southampton Docks

The liner docked as quarantine officials, led by Harold Brig watched on.

Harold Brig and several men walk up and across the gang plank to greet the Captain.

"Captain."

Brig shook the hand of the Captain, while wearing gloves.

"Sorry. Precautions," he smiled meekly.

People file past Quarantine. People in masks.

"Label your bags. Fill in the Quarantine forms," snapped a Quarantine officer.

The members of the Indian cricket team move forward in a line, led by C.K. Nayudu, followed by Amar Singh and Mohammad Nissar.

"I am Colonel Cottari Kanakaiya Nayudu and I demand you release us at once," demanded C.K. Nayudu.

"Label your bags. Fill in the Quarantine forms," continued the quarantine officer.

"I wish I could Colonel," said Harold Brig. "But the whole ship and crew have been placed under quarantine because of Cholera."

"I assure you whilst the service was less than standard," grumbled C.K. Nayudu, "I am perfectly fit and fine."

"Speak for yourself," said Mohammad Nissar.

"There is nothing I or anyone can do," said Harold Brig. "You have to stay here until we get the all clear."

"Label your bags. Fill in the Quarantine forms," the quarantine officer repeated over and over.

"This is outrageous," yelled C.K. Nayudu. "These conditions are appalling."

"No, they're called home for most of your servants back home C.K.," added Amar Singh to more laughter.

Chapter 7

"Laugh all you like you jackals. I am going to get out of here, one way or the other," grumbled C.K. Nayudu

"Label your bags. Fill in the Quarantine forms," repeated the quarantine officer.

****

Docks, Cargo Ship

The young cricketers led by Parindra Chamar shuffle down the gang plank onto the dock where Anthony De Mello was standing.

"Welcome to England! "

Gagan Nayanar was staring at the surroundings and bumps into Kanan Ram.

"Ow! Careful you oaf."

"Sorry."

"Grab all your luggage, we are on the 11 O'Clock train to Manchester and can't be late. Your first match is tomorrow against the United Coal Miners Cricket Team."

"So follow me."

The young men follow De Mello to a waiting bus and get on.

Wonderful Untouchables

Chapter 8

Westminster

Inside Westminster Palace. Prime Minister Ramsay MacDonald was walking out of the Commons with another Minister when Cecil Parker burst up to him. At first MacDonald was taken aback and grabbed his chest.

"For gods sake man!" yelled Ramsay MacDonald. "Do I have to have you gelded?"

"The Indians," whispered Cecil Parker. "They have been put in quarantine."

"Which Indians Parker?"

"The Indian Cricketers. Apparently there was an outbreak of Cholera on their ship and the whole passenger and crew list have been slapped into quarantine for a minimum of four to six weeks."

"Four to six weeks!" bellowed Ramsay MacDonald, causing everyone to stop and stare. "The test is in three weeks."

Ramsay MacDonald started rubbing his forehead as Lord Baldwin and Neville Chamberlain walked past.

"Everything alright Prime Minister?" smiled Lord Baldwin. "A glass of water? A tonic perhaps?"

Ramsay MacDonald composed himself and stared at Baldwin.

"All Fine Baldwin. Carry on," he replied.

Baldwin and others moved away as MacDonald grabbed Parker by the arm and dragged him to a corner.

"Get Gilmour or Stanley to get them out."

"Prime Minister, they are conservative members," said Cecil Parker. "They'll never budge. Besides, Quarantine laws are absolutely firm. If anything fishy is done, they'll be back to Baldwin like flies to -"

"Yes, yes. Got it. So what do we do?"

Cecil Parker shrugged his shoulders.

****

10 Downing Street

Inside the office of the Prime Minister, Ramsay MacDonald was reclining back in his chair with a towel over his forehead when Rose Rosenberg enters the room.

"Prime Minister, the Indian Cricket delegation is here to see you."

Chapter 8

Ramsay MacDonald let the towel drop from his forehead as he leant forward and got out of his chair, re-tightening his tie.

"Let them in."

Soon after the Maharaja of Porbandar and Grant Govan appeared, along with Lord John Sankey. Rose Rosenberg excused herself from the room.

"Your Highness," said Ramsay MacDonald reaching out to shake the hand of the Maharaja.

"Prime Minister," smiled the Maharaja.

"Mr Govan," said Ramsay MacDonald as he shook the hand of Grant Govan.

"Prime Minister," replied Grant Govan as Ramsay MacDonald signalled for the men to sit, while he returned to the chair behind his desk.

"Well it's over," moaned Ramsay MacDonald. "You may as well tell Mr Gandhi that this government will be lucky to last till the weekend and when Baldwin takes over, you can pretty much kiss the Round Table Negotiations goodbye as well."

"Prime Minister, I am here to play cricket, not to speak on behalf of M.K. Gandhi," replied the Maharaja. "Although I consider it an honour you would consider otherwise."

"That's the point. Bloody cricket," grumbled Ramsay MacDonald. "No Indian Cricket team, no test. No test, angry King, new Government, no constitution for India. Don't you see?"

"You're the Prime Minister of Great Britain," said Grant Govan. "Surely you can override quarantine and release the team?"

"And face the fire storm of media frenzy when I break the law over quarantine? I've got a media pack outside right now waiting to meet the India cricket team as a sign of good will. No thank you. The pitch forks are already sharp enough. No, I am afraid we're done for gentlemen."

"So an Indian cricket team in three weeks," said Grant Govan, rubbing his chin. "I mean a team of cricketers from India."

"You are the head official of cricket in India aren't you? " asked Ramsay MacDonald looking slightly nervous at the reaction of Grant Govan.

"Sure. Sure. I was just getting clear in my mind the problem. You just need an Indian cricket side."

"You mean to tell me you have another side tucked in your back pocket somewhere do you?"

"Well actually yes," smiled Grant Govan as the Maharaja of Porbandar looked over at Grant Govan who waved him down. At the same moment, Rose Rosenberg popped her head in and Ramsay MacDonald spotted her.

"Mr Jardine, the English Cricket Captain is outside Prime Minister," she smiled.

"Unless he is an Indian and plays first class cricket, he can wait," bellowed Ramsay MacDonald, waving at Rose Rosenberg.

"He was born in India," she quipped.

"Don't tempt me."

Rose Rosenberg closed the door.

"A team of Harijans," said Grant Govan.

"A team of what?"

"Dalits," added the Maharaja.

"In English if you would be so kind?" asked Ramsay MacDonald.

"Untouchables," said Grant Govan.

"What in the devil is a team of Untouchable cricketers doing here playing county cricket?"

"Not county cricket," replied Grant Govan. "They were invited by the unions and workers of Manchester and Liverpool to come and play. It was the idea of M. K. Gandhi."

"I am not so sure where you are going with this - "

"Nor am I -" said the Maharaja.

"Now, hold for a moment," said Grant Govan. "You... we each have our problems if this test does not go ahead. Lets just say for the sake of argument that the Harijans, the untouchables play as India, at least until the real team is clear. We can then rotate them out of the line up and none will be the wiser."

"The English cricketers will be the wiser," said the Maharaja.

"They only have to put on a civilised fight," smiled Grant Govan. "The match goes ahead. Indian Cricket is safe. The Round Table is a success. Everyone is happy."

"And the press outside?" asked Ramsay MacDonald.

"You have both your captains here," grinned Grant Govan. "Let them handle the press with you."

Ramsay MacDonald rubbed his chin for a moment.

****

10 Downing Street

While a swarm of media film and take photos, the Prime Minister Ramsay MacDonald was standing in the centre with the Maharaja of Porbandar and Douglas Jardine.

Chapter 8

"So, in the spirit of good will," smiled Ramsay MacDonald, "I welcome the captain of the All India team the Maharaja of Porbandar and our very own Douglas Jardine as captain of England who will meet at Lords at the end of June for the very first test between our peoples."

The press continued to take pictures with some reporters yelling out as all three men stand and smile.

Wonderful Untouchables

Chapter 9

Cricket Field, Manchester

The young men of the Sisters of Charity were fielding while the union cricket side were batting. Kanan Ram was bowling. He fired down a lightning fast delivery, shocking the batsman as his stumps went flying. A collective hurrah from the young Indians.

"Well done Kan!" yelled Chetan Sadna.

"The fastest of all India," yelled Sagar Khade.

"Hang on. Wait a minute what about me?" asked Gagan Nayanar.

Kanan Ram received the ball back and walked over to where Gagan was fielding, waiting for the new batsman to arrive.

"Don't worry Ga," added Kanan Ram ."You can have a go next Innings. Just give me a couple more overs."

As the cricket match continued, Grant Govan and Kumar Shri Limbdi along with the Maharaja of Porbandar arrived and greeted Anthony De Mello and David Caldwell who were already seated. When Caldwell saw the Maharaja and Govan, he got up, followed by De Mello and extended his hand.

"Your highness. It's an honour," said David Caldwell. "Wow, these young men are good."

Another shout in the background and the umpire lifted his finger yet again to signal another wicket taken. Grant Govan looked over at De Mello.

"Very good," smiled De Mello.

The Maharaja and Govan sat down and continued to watch the game, the Maharaja transfixed by the spectacle.

At the conclusion of the game, the young men of the Sisters of the Poor applauded the other team of union cricketers as they exit the field. Grant Govan, Kumar Shri Limbdi, the Maharaja of Porbandar and Anthony De Mello stepped onto the ground.

"Well done! Well done all of you," said De Mello.

"It was nothing. I was expecting some sort of distraction like canons, or a midfield marching band," smiled Gagan Nayanar. "But it was a fair match."

"We are kind of used to English teams back in India not playing fair," added Sagar Khade. "Especially the regimental teams."

Collective laughter.

"Boys, this is R.E. Grant Govan," said De Mello. "He is the President of Cricket of India."

Grant Govan started to shake their hands.

Chapter 9

"And this is the Maharaja of Porbandar, the Captain of the All India Cricket side," added De Mello.

A collective "ah" from the young men as they eagerly shake his hand.

"Outstanding men," smiled the Maharaja.

"Thank you, your highness," smiled Parindra.

"Boys," said Grant Govan. "I mean men. There is something of great importance we wish to discuss with you."

Suddenly Samir Saroj bursts into tears, quickly followed by Bhavesh Makwana.

"We are sorry sir. We did not mean to take them," they said as the boys continue to cry.

Grant Govan looked over at De Mello who shrugged his shoulders.

"What are you talking about?" asked De Mello, looking at the other players.

"The slippers from the hostel sir," said Samir Saroj. "We are sorry. We will put them back."

Grant Govan huffed and shook his head.

"I'm not talking about slippers. I'm talking about the future of cricket in India."

"Except for myself and Kumar, the whole Indian cricket team is in quarantine," said the Maharaja.

Another collective "ah" from the young cricketers.

"In any event under ordinary circumstances, we would simply wait for the quarantine to be lifted and re-schedule the games," continued the Maharaja.

"But these are no ordinary times," said Grant Govan.

"Right," said the Maharaja. "At the moment, there is a Second Round Table Conference scheduled in a few days, after which India was to play its first test."

"Men," said Grant Govan, "if we do not field a team as India at that test, then it could be the end of Cricket in India."

"How is that possible?" asked Parindra. "The British are still in control, cricket is everywhere."

"There are powerful forces who are working towards self rule who would like to see the end of Indians playing cricket and who would like nothing more for this upcoming test match with England to fail," added Grant Govan.

"You want us to play for India?" asked Gagan Nayanar.

"Your name is Gagan is it not?" said the Maharaja.

Gagan nods sheepishly.

"I saw in your bowling action Gagan, the brilliance of Amar Singh," smiled the Maharaja. "You even have the right height. With a bit of grooming, you could be like him."

Laughing amongst the young men.

"Your highness, Gagan like Singh," said Kanan Ram. "Are you serious?"

"Absolutely serious," smiled the Maharaja. "And your name is Kanan, correct?"

The laughing stopped.

"In you Kanan, I saw the speed and fire of the Mohammad Nissar," added the Maharaja.

The Maharaja then pointed to Parindra.

"And in you Parindra, I saw the brilliance of batting of C. K. Nayudu."

"He has the same sized head," added Sagar Khade, to collective laughing.

"Enough!" yelled Grant Govan. "This is serious. The future of cricket, maybe even the talks on independence, depend on India being represented at this test."

"But how?" asked Parindra. "How will we possibly pull something like this off? Even if we can bat, the English team and others know these people. We have never played at such a level."

"No one expects you to do miracles," answered Kumar Shri Limbdi. "Yet here you are. The gods have shined on you as boys now men who had never left Bombay, now in England, who had never met royalty, now standing to represent India. Your life, your path is full of miracles. All you have to do is continue to do what you have already been doing and we will take care of the rest."

Parindra Chamar looked over at Gagan Nayanar, then Chetann Sadna who nods and then all of the young men nod.

"For our country. For the love of cricket," smiled Parindra. "We are at your service."

Chapter 10

Southampton Docks

Usef Mamri was waiting on the docks as Kanan Mahar walked down the gang plank. Mamri shook his hand.

"I trust you had a pleasant voyage?" enquired Usef Mamri.

"I am only here to see Govan and De Mello fail and to support Dr Ambedkar with the Conference."

"Mohammad Al Soud and the All India Muslim League are arriving tomorrow," said Usef Mamri. "The Indian National Congress delegates are already here."

"When is the first match?"

"Against Sussex at Hove, then Marylebone and then the Test Match after the conference."

"Then I shall see how well they fare at Sussex, before planning our next move."

****

Savoy Hotel

The signature opulence of the The Savoy was as ever radiant as Grant Govan, Anthony De Mello, the

Maharaja of Porbandar and the young men arrived at the Hotel.

Once inside, midst the extraordinary interior beauty of the Hotel, they are greeted by the manager Sir Preston Scott and his staff.

"Your Highness, welcome," he smiled as he surveyed the faces of the young men of the Little Sisters of the Poor.

"Have the suites all been arranged?" asked the Maharaja.

Sir Preston Scott nodded approvingly.

"As you requested."

The Maharaja turned around to the young men.

"Then follow me."

As they walked through the luxury of The Savoy, their mouths were open in disbelief. The Maharaja of Porbandar and several of the young men led by Parindra Chamar entered an extraordinarily lavish suite of the Savoy.

"Is this a dream?" asked Parindra to the Maharaja.

"No, this is London," smiled the Maharaja. "And as you are representing your country, I wanted to show you where the gods sometimes reside."

"Is this there where the Indian side would normally stay?" asked Anan Ram.

Chapter 10

"You are blessed. It is the decision of his highness, the Maharaja that you stay here," added Grant Govan.

A Collective "ah" filled the surrounds.

"Don't get too comfortable, said the Maharaja. There will be practice tomorrow afternoon."

"But first," said Grant Govan, "some of us are visiting the team in Quarantine."

****

Quarantine Station

Grant Govan and the Maharaja of Porbandar walked through the depressing entrance of the Quarantine Station. They were escorted by the guards through to another steel door before being greeted by an unpleasantly officious nurse.

"You need to put these on before you meet the patients," she huffed, pointing to gowns and face masks. The nurse then handed them the full length gowns to put on.

Grant Govan and the Maharaja of Porbandar, wearing the gowns over their clothes, come to a reception area where the patients were divided by a barrier to the visitors. On the other side was the Indian cricket team.

"Get me out of here Govan," yelled C.K. Nayudu, "or I swear I'll ruin you and every other man who put this on me."

"Your not the only one. Anyway, there are much bigger issues afoot than worrying about your ego," replied Grant Govan. "Get closer, so I can speak with you all."

"When are we getting out of here?" asked Mohammad Nissar.

"I don't know," replied Grant Govan. "But the deeper issue is the future of Cricket in India and even maybe the self-rule movement."

"What do you mean?" asked Amar Singh.

"I met the Prime Minister of England with the Maharaja yesterday and he told us blankly that if the test does not go ahead then his career is finished and the conservatives will take control of government under Baldwin completely and then that will spell the end," said Grant Govan glumly.

"Then tell the Prime Minister of the United Kingdom to get us out of here. It is that simple," smiled C.K. Nayudu.

"He can't. That should be obvious already," said Grant Govan. "No, we have a plan. It should work."

"It will work," added the Maharaja.

Grant Govan nodded his head.

"Yes, you are right. It is going to work."

"What are you talking about Govan?" complained C.K. Nayudu. "You are speaking in tongues."

"We have another Indian cricket team that is temporarily filling in for you, in your place."

The faces of the Indian cricketers dropped to the ground.

"What? Who are these people? Please tell us," said Mohammad Nissar with frustration.

"Well, they are, not like you, they, are -"

"They are a Dalit team, here in England upon the request of M.K. Gandhi," interrupted the Maharaja. "And they are extraordinarily talented."

"So what you are telling us, is that you have replaced us with a team of untouchables?" growled C.K. Nayudu.

"In a word, yes," said Grant Govan.

"Now I am going to see you are finished," yelled C.K. Nayudu.

The Maharaja put up his hand and stopped the grumbling.

"Before you rush to condemn Mr Govan, may I be allowed to speak? I am the Maharaja of Porbander. I was borne into an elite and privileged life. In our culture, I was granted the extraordinary gift of being borne at the top. These young boys were not. Now, I know most of you have fought hard to make well for yourselves, through your talent and your character. So it makes sense that you feel upset with what you have heard. But let me remind you again what is at stake and how the universe has placed us in this teaching moment. Our future hangs in the balance, not with those borne to privilege, but those who were borne with nothing. And if you have any love for our country, which I am certain is true for all of you, you will find it in your heart to keep this quiet and to do everything to pray and support this succeeds until you are free."

The Indian cricketers looked at one another and then at the Maharaja as C.K. Nayudu shrugged his shoulders.

"Do we have any other choice?"

****

Practice With Maharaja

The young men of the Little Sisters of the Poor were on a cricket pitch waiting as the Maharaja of Porbandar and Kumar walked toward them.

"I was impressed what I saw at Manchester. But you will have to do a lot better than that to pull off the illusion you are the Indian cricket team."

The boys mumbled amongst themselves before the Maharaja pointed to Gagan Nayanar.

"Gagan, correct?"

Gagan nodded.

"Your action is not as fast as Kanan. But you can be more accurate. You will play the great cricketer Amar Singh."

The boys laugh.

"This is serious. Now concentrate on what I am saying," frowned the Maharaja. "And Kanan, you will be the fast bowler Mohammad Nissar."

The Maharaja then pointed to Sagar.

"Sagar, you will be Wazir Ali and Bhavesh you will be his brother Nazir."

He pointed to Parindra.

"And Parindra. You will be C.K. Nayudu."

A Collective "ohh" filled the air.

"Thanks," smiled Parindra.

"Of course Kumar and myself will be who we are. But all of you will have to remember not only the part you are playing, but to work much closer together. So lets get to practise."

Gagan Nayanar and Kanan Ram take turns to bowl to the other young men.

"Cricket is a game of the mind, a test of wit and skill," yelled the Maharaja. "It is not the most talented batsman that succeeds, but the one who can keep his focus, without all the distractions around him."

The Maharaja walked over to Gagan Nayanar.

"Do not be fearful of the stumps, nor of bowling a full length. Let the batsman earn his runs, in the hope that he will tire and edge to being caught."

Chapter 11

Sussex County Cricket Field

Grant Govan, De Mello, the Maharaja of Porbandar, Kumar Shri Limbdi and the young men of the Little Sisters of the Poor arrived at the Sussex County Cricket Ground.

"Remember what we discussed. Today not only are you embodying your heroes. You *are* your heroes."

"And for goodness sake, don't break character," added Grant Govan.

"For Parindra as C. K. Nayudu that will be easy," quipped Sagar Khade.

Collective laughing erupted amongst the young men.

"This is serious," frowned the Maharaja. "It is not just my reputation but the reputation of the people you are representing. Do not treat this lightly."

The mood returned to sombre as the Captain of the Sussex Team (M.W. Tate) stepped over.

"Your highness, welcome!" smiled the Captain M.W. Tate.

"Thank you for your invitation," smiled the Maharaja.

"Someone had to get you out into the bright fresh air," grinned the Captain, before an awkward silence.

"I must say, your team looks in remarkably good shape," said M.W. Tate, trying to recover. "The fountain of youth!"

"They will well and truly make up for it on the pitch Tate," replied the Maharaja.

Tate laughed.

"Shall we flip a coin then to see who bats first?" asked M.W. Tate.

"After you," smiled the Maharaja.

M. W. Tate flipped a coin.

"We lose. Well I guess it is up to you."

The Maharaja of Porbandar looked up at the sky and then across to the team. "Today. I think we shall start by batting," he smiled.

****

Sussex County Cricket Stands

Usef Mamri arrived at the Sussex County team stand and found a space next to some British spectators. As he sat down, Anthony De Mello spotted him from afar.

"How have the Indians been playing?" asked Usef Mamri of a nearby British spectator.

"Wonderfully well," smiled the spectator. "They made 236. That Limbdi fellow was wonderful as was C. K. Nayudu. Now this Mohammad Nissar is bowling superbly."

Usef looked out to the ground.

"But that is not Mohammad Nissar."

"Oh. Then who is he?" asked the spectator, a little surprised.

****

Sussex County Cricket

The Maharaja of Porbandar was congratulating the young men after the game as the Sussex County team left the field. Grant Govan and De Mello walk over to where the team was standing.

"A draw is still a wonderful achievement to you all," said the Maharaja. "Well done."

"You were all brilliant," bubbled Grant Govan.

Suddenly Usef Mamri appeared bounding onto the field.

"Except, I do not know who these people are," he grumbled menacingly.

"Mr Mamri what an unexpected surprise!" said De Mello, pretending to be surprised.

"What is going on?" said Usef Mamri.

"Excuse me gentlemen," grimaced Grant Govan, "this is one of our board of Cricket."

Grant Govan, De Mello and the Maharaja steered Usef Mamri away from the main group and closer to the exit to the team change rooms.

"Who are these people?" repeated Usef Mamri . "They certainly are not the Indian cricket side!"

"Settle Mamri. I know we have some differences."

"I am not talking about differences, I am talking about fraud."

"Sir, I assure you I am the Maharaja of Porbandar and I take offence to your imputations. Now, if you have something to say, you can say it to me. Otherwise, I suggest you speak to the President and the Secretary in private."

Grant Govan grabbed Usef Mamri by the arm and dragged him off the field and into the team changing rooms to the side.

"Lets have a chat Usef, shall we?"

Chapter 12

The Savoy

The magnificent Savoy Hotel. Inside the Maharaja's suite, Grant Govan was tying up Usef Mamri to a beautiful chair as Anthony De Mello looked on.

"I swear when I am finished, you will never work for cricket again," growled Usef Mamri. "In fact I will make it my solemn mission that there is no cricket in India, period."

"I can't believe we kidnapped him," said De Mello.

"What other choice did I have?" replied Grant Govan. "He was going to blow the whole thing."

"You are mad," interrupted Usef Mamri. "Both of you. You will never get away with it."

Grant Govan grabbed a piece of cloth and gagged Usef who initially struggled.

"Sorry Usef. It is for own good. Don't worry. It's the best room service you'll ever eat."

"At least until we work out how we will get out of this mess."

****

Second Round Table Conference

Outside the location for the Second Round Table Conference on India and Self Governance the delegates of the Indian National Congress, including Mahatma Gandhi, were welcomed by British Officials in front of the conference hall. A mass of media photograph and film the event.

A news announcer spoke into a microphone while observing the arrival of the delegates. "*The Government today welcomed delegates from the India National Congress led by Mr Gandhi and other parties to the Second Round Table Conference on the future of self governance for India.*"

Another wave of Indian delegates arrived in the form of Mohammad Al Soud and members of the All India Muslim League. They were quickly joined by Dr B.D. Ambedkar accompanied by Kanan Mahar and others of the United Dalit Party.

The news announcer continued. "*Mr Mohammad Al Soud and other members of the All India Muslim League have just arrived. So too has arrived Dr B.D. Ambedkar accompanied by Kanan Mahar and others of the United Dalit Party. Dr B.D. Ambedkar represents the working classes of India, known as the Untouchables."*

Dr Ambedkar and Mohammad Al Soud stood outside the conference hall, smiling for the media.

"So have you seen Usef?" whispered Mohammad Al Soud.

"No. Kanan Mahar has also been looking for him," replied Dr Ambedkar.

Both men continued smiling for the cameras.

****

Practice Field

The Maharaja of Porbandar was standing on a field surrounded by the young men in a circle.

"Now tomorrow, we play the Marylebone Cricket Club and it will be the first time you get to see Lords, the hallowed home of Cricket."

A collective "ah" from the team.

"Make no mistake. This is a very strong side. Many of the players are the same as the English cricket team. So you will need to bring your best game."

"And I shall get to bowl on the most sacred field of cricket," said Gagan Nayanar.

"If your ego can fit through the gates," added Chetan Sadna.

Laughter.

"Be serious. Look at where we are," said Parindra. "Look at who is helping us! How many of us made up stories to each other that one day we would see how the great gods lived? How many of us thought about what life would be like if we lived like a real Maharaja? Now we have the most excellent teacher and we make jokes. No more jokes. We are not boys anymore. We are men!"

"Well said Parindra," smiled the Maharaja. "Thank you."

"No. Thank you, your highness."

****

Lords Oval

The Indian team headed by the Maharaja arrived at the gates of the Lords oval and then walked inside.

****

Marylebone Cricket Match

The match got underway as the young side stepped onto the ground to polite applause, followed by the Marylebone Cricket team.

Kanan Mahar was sitting in the members stand, next to a number of spectators including Ronald Waterhouse as the teams came out to shake each others hands.

"Ronald Waterhouse," smiled Ronald Waterhouse, introducing himself.

He extended his hand to Kanan Mahar.

"Kanan Mahar from the Indian cricket Board."

"Ah. So good luck today then. I hear your side has some pretty good bowlers."

"Yes. While I am on the board. I must confess, I am not overly interested in the result, other than the impact in discussions with the conference. If I had my way, our people would pay more interest in a non-British sport."

"Sounds like my boss," smiled Ronald Waterhouse. "He can't really stand this sport either."

De Mello and Grant Govan entered the stand and suddenly spotted Kanan Mahar. They move quickly over to him as India won the toss and decided to bat.

Meanwhile, Ronald Waterhouse spotted Cecil Parker sitting to the side.

"Cecil what are you doing here? Shouldn't you be with the PM taking care of all those delegates at the moment?"

"The Round Table Conference is fine. Can't I enjoy a game of cricket?"

Just then Grant Govan and Anthony De Mello arrive to where Kanan Mahar was sitting. As they moved across they noticed Cecil Parker, who acknowledged them briefly with a nod, that Ronald Waterhouse caught. Kanan didn't get up when he saw both Grant Govan and De Mello.

"Have you seen Usef Mamri?"

"No. Have you Anthony?"

"No Kanan."

"Strange. He said he was going down to watch the game at Sussex," said Kanan Mahar, "and I haven't heard from him since."

"I am sure he is fine and will turn up," smiled Grant Govan meekly.

Applause as the Marylebone team caught another wicket.

"Two for sixty two. Not looking good," said Ronald Waterhouse.

Chapter 12

"Who is up now?" asked Kanan Mahar.

"I think it is your man C.K. Nayudu. Quite famous. Even I have heard of his career."

Kanan stared out at the figure of Parindra Chamar dressed like C.K. Nayudu walking to the crease.

"That's not C.K. Nayudu."

Kanan Mahar swung around and looked squarely at Grant Govan and Anthony De Mello.

"What in the hell is going on?"

"Kanan if you give us a few minutes in the team rooms," smiled Grant Govan, "we can explain."

Kanan agreed and followed Grant Govan and De Mello out of the stands as Ronald Waterhouse looked over at the figure of Cecil Parker looking panicked.

****

Savoy Suite

Inside, Grant Govan was tying up Kanan Mahar next to Usef Mamri as Anthony De Mello looked on.

"Now we really are in deep trouble," mumbled De Mello.

"What else are we to do?"

"You are finished," said Kanan Mahar. "All of you. When Dr Ambedkar hears about this outrage."

"When Mohammad Al Soud hears about it as well," added Usef Mamri. "I swear when I am finished, you will never work for cricket again. In fact when he is President of an independent India, he will make sure that that there is no cricket in India, period."

"I can't believe we kidnapped him," said De Mello

"He was going to blow the whole thing," replied Grant Govan.

Suddenly, the Maharaja of Porbandar and Kumar Shri Limbdi entered the room and see Grant Govan and Anthony De Mello tying up Kanan Mahar.

"My goodness, what are you doing?" asked the Maharaja.

"Your highness, we had no choice," said Grant Govan.

"We always have a choice Mr Govan."

"Get us out of here," said Kanan Mahar, "and we will say you had nothing to do with our kidnapping your highness."

"This will end cricket for good in India," growled Usef Mamri. "The All Muslim League will sure of it. But you will not be in the trouble as these two."

Chapter 12

"Now, wait a moment," said the Maharaja. "You both are members of the Cricket Board of India, why would you want to see it destroyed?"

"It is bourgeois British," grumbled Kanan Mahar. "It is a colonial dinosaur."

"It is a necessary sacrifice to our independence," added Usef Mamri.

"You mean you'd just as soon see it cease for political reasons, but you have no opinion of it and yet you are on the board?" sighed the Maharaja.

"It is a pleasant pursuit. It does not offend our religion," grinned Usef Mamri.

"And you Mr Mahar?" asked the Maharaja.

"I'd much prefer something with more action, some physical contact. At least rugby has some blood," smiled Kanan Mahar.

"See what I mean," said Grant Govan. "They're mad. That's why - "

The Maharaja put up his hand as he grabbed a chair and sits in front of the two men tied up.

"Alas an eye for an eye makes the whole world blind," said the Maharaja.

"Shakespeare?" asked Usef Mamri.

"Gandhi," replied the Maharaja. "Gentlemen, why do you think I love cricket? Why do you think these young men from nothing love cricket?"

Both men shrugged their shoulders.

"Because it is the only sport that combines all the skill and tactics of warfare and none of the bloodshed," continued the Maharaja. "In fact, the colour is white, the sign of peace. Certainly there is the game of polo. A game invented by our collective ancestors in the high country from the heads of the slain enemy. Or soccer or rugby, also celebrated from the heads of the unfortunate. But cricket demands the wisest of mind, the deepest of culture and the most civil of discourse."

"I have never understood it," said Usef Mamri.

"And yet you ridicule what you do not understand," added the Maharaja. "Gentlemen, we play cricket in the slums and in the gardens of India, not because of England. We play cricket because we are Indians. Because our culture has survived a hundred invasions from before Alexander the Great. We play, because we know we are at least equal."

The Maharaja got up from his chair and walked over to Grant Govan and then Anthony De Mello away from the two men tied up.

Chapter 12

"While I do not approve of your methods Mr Govan. Until the conference is concluded and the Test Match is over, see to it these men are discretely kept out of sight," said the Maharaja. "Possibly, my ship instead of such a famous hotel and staff perhaps?"

Grant Govan and De Mello nodded in approval.

"What did he say?" yelled Kanan Mahar. "What did he say?"

Wonderful Untouchables

Chapter 13

Second Round Table Conference

Lord Baldwin entered the hallway during the conference as Indian and British delegates were deep in conversations in different corners. As soon as Ronald Waterhouse spotted Lord Baldwin, he signalled for him to come over to him.

"What is it?" said Lord Baldwin. "I received your cryptic note. I was having a fine nap in there."

"There is something off with the Indian team," said Ronald Waterhouse excitedly.

"Humour like reason, does ill suit you Waterhouse."

"I mean sir, I was at Lords and some of the Indian cricket officials were arguing that the people playing were imposters. Cecil Parker and the PM seems to be in on it. I have heard now that Members of the Muslim delegation and the Untouchables have gone missing."

Lord Baldwin rubbed his chin.

"So they should after the last screw up of the Round Table. What are you saying? That they're hiding something?"

"All I know is that the prime enemy of the Indian National Congress wants to meet you on a subject they say is of the highest confidence and utmost importance."

"So the enemy of my enemy seeks to prove the truth of such a maxim then? So be it! Make it happen."

****

Quarantine, Reception Area

At the quarantine station, Grant Govan and the Maharaja of Porbandar were meeting again with the Indian cricket side.

"One more week, possibly two and you will all be out," said Grant Govan.

"But the test is this Saturday after the close of the conference," protested Amar Singh.

"This is the most degrading experience in my life," moaned C.K. Nayudu.

"You should be proud of those young men," replied the Maharaja. "The second draw, against a far superior side. Parindra Chamar who is playing as you C.K. top scored against Marylebone at 118 not out."

"That is the least he could do," huffed C.K. Nayudu.

"You should never have allowed this to happen," grumbled Mohammad Nissar.

"You know what? You are all wrong," frowned the Maharaja. "Today I saw men, men who are cricket officials put politics, money and religion above a game for which they know nothing about and have little care. Meanwhile, I saw young men. Honourable men, who gave everything not for fame, or glory but for the love of the game; the love of cricket."

"They do it because they're told what to do," grumbled C.K. Nayudu.

General laughter.

"You still don't get it do you?" replied the Maharaja. "This is not about cricket. It is about the future of India. The talks hang in the balance. There are people of the same mind as those who see the end of cricket in India that would be more than happy for the talks to fail. You all say you're patriots. But when you slander these young boys, who are doing this and against all their fears, then you are not. Shame on you. Shame on all of you for being on your high horses when India needs you more than ever to come together."

"Maybe you should be at the talks," added Amar Singh.

General laughter.

"You'd make a convincing politician your highness," grinned C.K. Nayudu.

The Maharaja of Porbandar shook his head and then looks at Grant Govan.

"Let's go," said Grant Govan. "Your talking to a brick wall."

Chapter 14

Round Table Conference

The Prime Minister Ramsay MacDonald was sitting at a central table between the two sides of delegates as a speaker finished. There was mute applause. Lord Baldwin seized the moment.

"Mr Chairman," yelled Lord Baldwin. "A point of order. Mr Chairman."

"Order," yelled Ramsay MacDonald.

"The Chair recognizes the Right Honourable Lord Baldwin."

"Thank you Prime Minister. My point of order is really a point of order of recognition to our honourable colleagues and delegates from India. As it has come to my attention that there is not just one illustrious touring team of cricketers from India upon our shores, but two."

Muffled conversation.

"Order. Now Lord Baldwin, if -"

"Prime Minister," said Lord Baldwin, interrupting the Prime Minister. "If I am allowed to speak?"

Calls from both sides to let him speak. The Prime Minister sat down and starts to rub his forehead.

"As I was saying," smiled Lord Baldwin. "It has come to my attention that there is a second side of illustrious cricketers from India who have come by invitation. However, these are no ordinary cricketers. Indeed, they are what is known as untouchables, from the poorest streets of India. I propose as a gesture of goodwill that they be permitted during the lunch break at the historic Test Match between India and England to provide a demonstration. Do I have a seconder."

"I second this splendid proposition to celebrate peace in our time," blurted Neville Chamberlain.

"Not now Neville," growled Lord Baldwin, before he looked back at Ramsay MacDonald.

"Prime Minister?"

Ramsay MacDonald looked nervous. The Prime Minister looked at the Indian side who were all holding up their hands as well as were the British behind Lord Baldwin.

"Very well. The motion is passed by unanimous consent and will be forwarded to Lords to arrange. Now, if we can return to the agenda of the proceedings."

"Thank you Prime Minister," grinned Lord Baldwin.

Chapter 14

****

The Savoy

Inside the Maharaja's suite at the Savoy, the Maharaja of Porbandar, Grant Govan and Cecil Parker were deep in conversation, while the young team of the Little Sisters of the Poor look on.

"Unless you can magically produce another team, then we're done," said Cecil Parker.

He rubbed his head.

"Even if you produce a team at lunch," continued Cecil Parker, "and Baldwin exposes this team as not the Indian team it's over."

"Plus the two pigeons stowed away on your boat your highness," added Grant Govan.

"What is he talking about?" asked Cecil Parker.

"Nothing," smiled the Maharaja. "It's just two cricket officials we have temporarily kidnapped."

"I knew it," moaned Cecil Parker. "Now I am definitely going to prison."

"Calm down," said the Maharaja. "If destiny has taken us this far, then I refuse to believe this is the end."

"But what if it is the end?" asked Cecil Parker. "What if there is no miracle?"

Parindra Chamar stepped forward into the conversation.

"We have no hope then of representing our nation with dignity tomorrow," said Parindra.

"My father before he died told me of a story when he was a young boy at school at Rajkot," said the Maharaja. "He remembered meeting another student whose family had a long history of being the loyal prime ministers and administrators of the kingdom held by our family. Yet he was not a great sportsman, nor overly social. Then one day, some older boys were picking on him and my father felt it a sense of duty to come and protect him. Instead, this boy thanked my father and said he would be fine. That if he approached the bullies with respect and honour, then they would eventually see the error of their behaviour."

"What happened?" asked Chetan Sadna.

"Well, this boy was beaten senseless and if not for my father adding his fists, he would have been finished. In any event, my father never forgot the courage of that boy in the face of adversity."

"What was his name?" asked Kanan Ram.

"His name was Mahatma Gandhi."

Chapter 14

A collective "ah" from the young men.

"You see, sometimes you don't have to win, to win," smiled the Maharaja. "Sometimes you only have to stand and take the blows to be heroes."

"But this is the English Cricket team and a very public demonstration. They will crush us," said Parindra.

"They will expose us and arrest us," added Cecil Parker.

"Do you think it is chance that these amazing events happened?" asked the Maharaja. "As Indians, surely you must place some faith in the beliefs of your ancestors, who believed everything was according to a great divine plan."

The Maharaja looked over at Chetan Sadna.

"To you Chetan. You may have been borne in difficult circumstances."

"Yes your highness," smiled Chetan. "My mother gave birth to me and then handed me to my sister so she could get back to work at the washing stalls."

"And you Gagan. Your name means sky and heaven, while you Sagar, your name means ocean."

Collective laughter from the boys.

"Gagan as heaven. To the girls I don't think so."

Gagan hits him on the arm.

"Ow."

"What does my name mean? What does Kanan mean?" asked Kanan Ram.

"Your name means nosy rabbit," smiled the Maharaja.

General laughter.

"No Kanan, your name means Forest."

The Maharaja looks over at Parindra.

"And Parindra your name means the Lion."

Collective "ah" from the assembled team.

"Heaven ordained this moment," said the Maharaja. "The gods chose you to be here, to play here. This is your moment. This is your time. You can win. You have already won the hardest battle. Take this moment and do not doubt yourself one instant. You are my sons, you are my brothers. You can do wonderful things. You are the living paradox, the Wonderful Untouchables."

Chapter 15

Lords

Grant Govan, De Mello, the Maharaja of Porbandar, Kumar Shri Limbdi and the young men of the Little Sisters of the Poor arrived at Lords.

"You played here the other day so there is nothing to worry about," smiled Kumar Shri Limbdi to the boys.

"Sure. Tell that to my stomach and the thousands of people here," replied Gagan Nayanar.

The ground was indeed packed full of spectators ready to watch the historic match, including almost all of the delegates from the round table conference, including Ramsay MacDonald and Lord Baldwin.

Upon the arrival of King George and the playing of the anthem, the audience and players stood to attention.

In a small booth, behind the members stand, an announcer accounted for the game: "*A beautiful day here at Lords as Douglas Jardine and the Maharaja of Porbandar meet on the pitch to toss a coin and see who will bat.*"

A coin was tossed by Jardine, before the umpires inspected its fall.

"Jardine won the toss, so England will bat first."

The Maharaja of Porbandar shook hands with the umpires before the rest of the side came onto the field. Kanan picked up the ball and lined himself up to bowl.

"Nissar bowls and Holmes deflects down leg side with Sutcliffe for a single."

Kanan gets the ball handed to him by Parindra Chamar and then prepares to bowl again."

"Nissar bowls again and Sutcliffe is caught out on 3 runs and England is 1 for 8."

The team was ecstatic and congratulated Kanan. They composed themselves as the next English batsman came to the crease.

****

Lords Stand

In the members stand, Ramsay MacDonald was watching along with Cecil Parker and Lord John Sankey.

"Not a bad bowler after all. So far, so good," smiled Lord John Sankey.

Chapter 15

"Wait till lunch," sighed Ramsay MacDonald. "That's Baldwin's feast."

****

Lords Field

The young men continued fielding against the English team, as the commentator described the events:

"*Nissar bowls again and Holmes is caught out on 6 runs and England is 2 for 11. A Shaky start for the side.*"

Gagan Nayanar now began his spell of bowling, pretending to be Singh.

"*Singh bowls again and Woolley is run out. England is now 3 for 19.*"

Jardine and Hammond continued to fire shots across the ground until they were also given out.

"*Jardine and Hammond have steadied the English side.*"

Finally, the last English wicket fell.
"*England is all out for 259. What a tremendous result by the Indians. And now, for a special presentation by his majesty King George V.*"

Wonderful Untouchables

****

Lords Ground, Kings Presentation

King George stepped onto the ground, accompanied by Ramsay MacDonald, Lord John Sankey and Lord Baldwin. Grant Govan, Anthony De Mello and the Maharaja of Porbandar also come onto the ground.

On one side was the English cricket team and a separate team of the English Coal mining cricket team. On the other side was the Indian team but no sign of their opposites working class team from India.

"This is it," whispered Grant Govan to the Maharaja. "The End."

Robert Mallory directed the King into position. "Your majesty, first you will present to the Coal Mining team then the Dalit," he said.

"Yes, yes, another bloody speech," grumbled the King, before looking back at Robert Mallory. "The what?"

"The untouchables," whispered Robert Mallory.

Chapter 15

"For gods sake man," yelled Lord Baldwin. "Tell his majesty the truth."

"What are you talking about?" bellowed the King.

"The real Indian team is in -"

As Lord Baldwin was trying to finish his sentence, from the dressing rooms out stepped the real C.K. Nayudu, followed by Mohammad Nissar, Amar Singh, the Ali brothers and the rest of the team that had been in quarantine.

"Quarantine."

Grant Govan and Anthony De Mello looked at each other, as did the Maharaja of Porbandar.

The King looked at the players having arrived and shook his head.

"A bit tardy", he said. "Nonetheless we are all hear now, so lets get on with it shall we?"

C. K. Nayudu stood next to Parindra Chamar.

"Thank you for not injuring my reputation," whispered C. K. Nayudu to Parindra.

"Thank you for saving all of us," smiled Parindra.

"But your majesty. These men are imposters," protested Lord Baldwin.

"I assure you sir," frowned the Maharaja, "I am the Maharaja of Porbandar."

"Not you," yelled Lord Baldwin, pointing at the boys, "them."

"Baldwin, what the hell are you still babbling about?" said the King.

"These men are the untouchables," said Lord Baldwin pointing to the boys, "and the others are the real Indian cricketers."

"Now Baldwin, I am warning you," said the King, "you have thirty seconds to explain yourself before I reinstitute castration as a Royal Prerogative."

"Yes your Majesty," smiled Lord Baldwin. "The team you see before you claiming to be the Indian cricket team, are in fact imposters. Whereas the real cricket team is in fact the claimed Untouchables."

"Damn it man. The more you speak, the less sense you make," grumbled the King.

"They kidnapped me to hush it up," yelled Usef Mamri.

"And they kidnapped me too," added Kanan Mahar.

"Is this true McDonald?" asked the King. "What do you have to say for yourself."

"Yes your Majesty," replied Ramsay MacDonald, bowing his head. "Not the part about kidnapping. I had nothing to do with any such thing. But the point made by Baldwin that the Indian team are the untouchables and the untouchables are the Indian team."

"I am the true Maharaja of Porbandar and the true Captain of the Indian cricket team," said the Maharaja.

"Now I really do have a headache," sighed the King. "Can't anyone please sort this mess out for me?"

Mahatma Gandhi appeared onto the field, and smiled to everyone present.

"Allow me to explain it to your Majesty," he said. "A true son of India is a Muslim, a Hindu, a Christian, a Buddhist, a Jain. He is a Brahman but more he is a Child of God. This truth is expressed most eloquently by what we have witnessed today, where a man born to privilege is proud to call those born with almost nothing as brothers. Where men born to wealth are prepared for the sake of their people to be humble and known as the simplest and poorest. Your majesty, when you measure the strength of India and our determination to decide our own fate, look then to our people and what unites us, what makes us who we are."

"Why can't someone write me a speech half as good as that," replied the King. "Well Mr Gandhi. You'll have your own parliament as equal and fair representation. But be careful what you wish for. If you think fighting for freedom is tough. Wait till you have to manage the peace."

****

So it was that the Maharaja of Porbandar helped improve the lives of hundreds of thousands of working poor throughout Porbandar and India.
India gained its independence. And the game of Cricket survived and thrived in India.

www.ingramcontent.com/pod-product-compliance
Lightning Source LLC
Chambersburg PA
CBHW082249120626
46555CB00009B/3012

* 9 7 8 1 6 4 4 1 9 0 0 4 3 *